HAPPY BIRTHDAY EVERYONE!

SHARRON ALLEN

Illustrated By Earline Gayle Escalona

To order additional copies of this book, contact:
Xlibris
1-888-795-4274
www.Xlibris.com
Orders@Xlibris.com

This book is for my brother Stevie, with love.
(Stephen Geoffrey Allen)

HAPPY BIRTHDAY
EVERYONE!

Today's a very special day
I heard my mother say.
A special gift, a special cake,
today is my birthday!

Today I am no longer four.
Today I'm *five* years old!
I wonder why we count the years . . .
I've never really been told.

My mom and dad - they count the years.
They know how old they are.
I have to ask their age because
it's hard to count that far!

I know how old my good friends are
'cause they have birthdays too.
And they all know how old *I* am.
Now just how old are *you*?

How old are all the things I see
outside my window here?
Do they have birthdays and do they
keep counting every year?

Here by my window - see this tree,
and there the flowers and rocks?
Do they have parties with a cake
and gifts wrapped in a box?

Nesting high in this maple tree,
new baby robins call.
Do they know when their birthdays are,
or are they way too small?

The sun is shining on my face
like it has done before.
Has it ever had a birthday cake
with candles from the store?

Does that blue sky I see up high
remember its birthday?
Do passing clouds or sparkling stars?
I've never heard them say.

Tonight when I am tucked in bed
and out my window see
the moon sail by, I'll ask out loud,
"Are you as old as me?"

An owl lives near the river there;
I hear her call "hoo-hooooo."
Is she wishing a friend of hers
a happy birthday too?

Oh look! The geese fly in a 'vee'
across the sky so high.
Their honks must be a birthday song
for some goose turning five!

And what about my feathered friends
whose homes are at the zoo?
Do macaws know the birthday song?
Do ostrich and emus?

Do toucans, penguins and trogons,
cotingas, cockatoos,
have fun and sing to celebrate?
I surely hope they do!

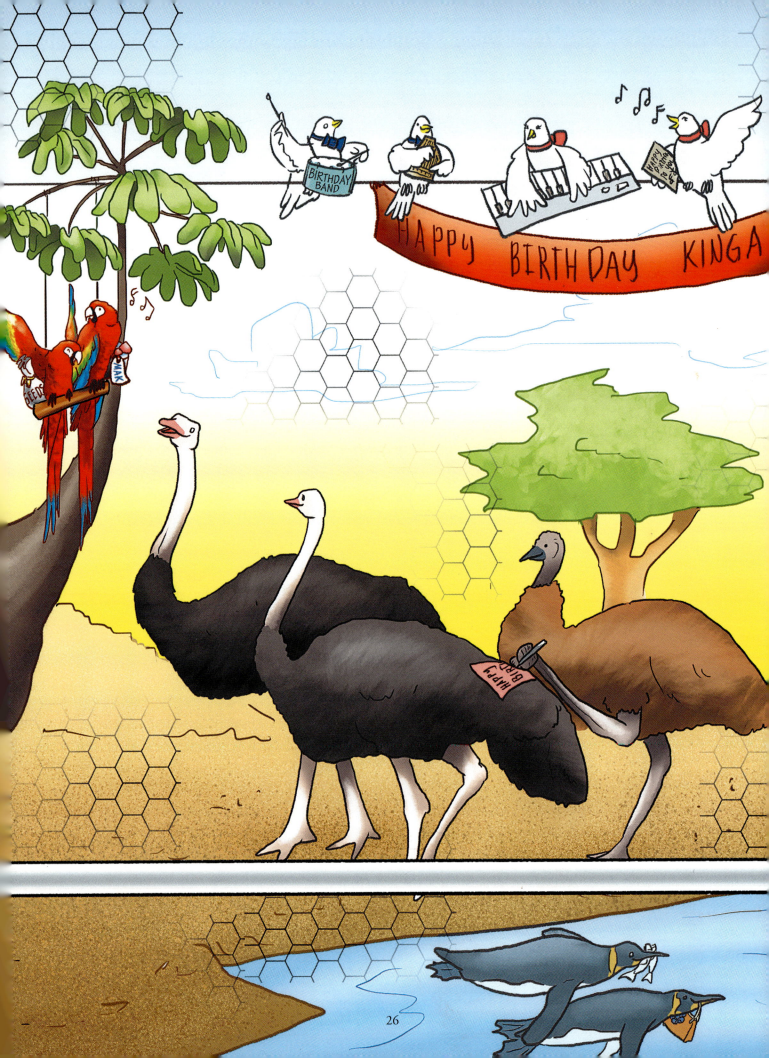

The long-necked giraffe lives at the zoo;
so does the polar bear.
I wonder if they know their age;
I wonder if they care.

Or elephants with their long trunks
and great big fan-shaped ears.
I've heard they live a very long time.
Can they count all their years?

The hippopotamus is huge -
I wonder if she dances.
On her birthday, I'd dance with her -
my toes would take their chances!

Do monkeys and orangutans,
baboons and chimpanzees,
have parties with banana cake
away up in the trees?

32

I saw the big cats at the zoo,
the cheetah face to face.
Do they play special birthday games?
I know who'd win a race!

When I ran home across the field,
some butterflies chased me.
Then dragonflies joined in our game –
t'was like a birthday party!

I wonder about that snake I saw
go slithering through the grass.
Does he know when to call his friends
for his own birthday bash?

The rabbits who play in the field
come to our garden to eat.
Are carrots, beans and lettuce leaves
their special birthday treats?

And what about the small creatures
like ants and bees and bugs?
Do all their legs and wings and things
get caught in birthday hugs?

Do rats and mice and voles and moles
who scurry about so fast,
take time for birthdays and slow down
to make their parties last?

The bats hang upside down in trees
and only play at night.
Do they have parties in the dark?
They give me such a fright!

And in the rivers, streams and lakes,
live trout and bass and catfish.
I wonder if they celebrate
with ice cream in a dish?

In oceans, do the manta rays
or sharks with many teeth,
have birthday parties with their friends
down at the coral reef?

The humpback whales who live at sea,
dive deep and for so long.
They're famous for the songs they sing.
Is one a birthday song?

Thinking about a birthday song,
reminds me: very soon
my friends will be here at my door.
My party starts at noon.

When they get here, I'll ask my friends
who live on Janssen's farm,
"Have you seen birthday parties there
around the big red barn?"

Does the cow give some milk to drink,
the horse give rides for fun?
Do the lambs share their birthday cake,
pigs serve hot-dogs on buns?

I wonder when we hear at dawn
that "cock-a-doodle-doo,"
if the rooster's singing in his way,
"Happy Birthday to you!"

Oh! There goes Mickey, my friend's cat.
He's off to run and play.
Does Mickey know how old he is
and when it's his birthday?

Now here comes Boo; I call his name,
and my dog barks a "Hi!"
On his birthday he'll get a gift.
Do you think Boo knows why?

I heard the doorbell ring and know
my friends have all come in.
They're calling "Happy Birthday!" now.
My party's to begin.

We'll all have fun with toys and games,
ice cream and birthday cake.
But first there's something I must do,
a wish that I must make:

May *everything* and *everyone*,
no matter what or who,
know just how old they really are
and have a birthday too!

Edwards Brothers Malloy
Oxnard, CA USA
July 28, 2015